Going on a Journey to the Sea

Written by
Jane Barclay

Illustrated by
Doris Barrette

Lobster Press ™

Barclay, Jane, 1957-
Going on a Journey to the Sea
Text © 2002 Jane Barclay
Illustrations © 2002 Doris Barrette

Published by Lobster Press™
1620 Sherbrooke Street West, Suites C & D, Montréal, Québec H3H 1C9
Tel. (514) 904-1100 • Fax (514) 904-1101
www.lobsterpress.com

Publisher: Alison Fripp
Edited by Jane Pavanel
Book design by Marielle Maheu

Distribution:
In the United States
Advanced Global Distribution Services
5880 Oberlin Drive
San Diego, CA 92121

In Canada
Raincoast Books
9050 Shaughnessey Street
Vancouver, BC V6P 6E5

We acknowledge the financial support of the Government of Canada through the Book Publishing Industry Development Program (BPIDP) for our publishing activities.

We acknowledge the support of the Canada Council for the Arts for our publishing program.

The Canada Council   Le Conseil des Arts
for the Arts   du Canada

SODEC
SOCIÉTÉ DE DÉVELOPPEMENT
DES ENTREPRISES CULTURELLES
Québec

National Library of Canada cataloguing in publication data

Barclay, Jane, 1957-
    Going on a journey to the sea

ISBN 1-894222-34-2

I. Barrette, Doris II. Title.

PS8553A74327G64 2002   jC813'.54 C2001-900048-0
PZ7.B37G64 2002

The illustrations were rendered in watercolors
The text was typeset in Sassoon Primary

Printed and bound in Hong Kong, China, by Book Art Inc, Toronto

To my parents, Thelma and Doug, who showed me the sea,
and to Andrew, Marge, Sue and Audrey, who shared the journey
Jane Barclay

To Elliot
Doris Barrette

I'm going on a journey with my sister to the sea
We packed a big red suitcase and a knapsack just for me
We're bringing suntan lotion and a blanket for the sand
I hold the pail and shovel and my sister holds my hand

"All aboard, your tickets please," clickety-clickety-clickety-clack
We're riding on a shiny train that's swaying down the track
Fields of flowers nod their heads as birds go swooping by
We've never, ever seen the sea, my sister Meg and I

We're bouncing on an old gray bus, a jiggly, giggly pair
A teasing breeze is blowing in and playing with my hair

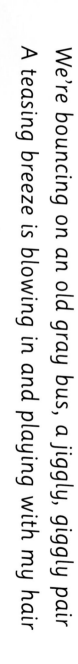

We count the cows and horses, then we sing a traveling song
I wonder, "Are we there yet, Meg?" The road winds on and on

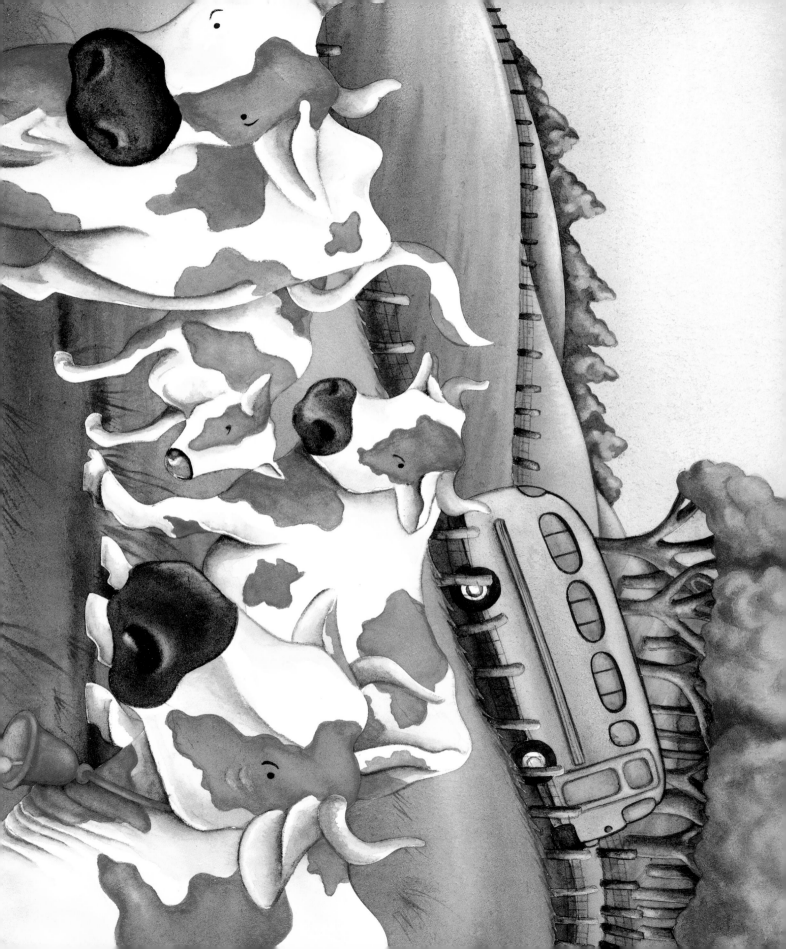

We're biking past a shallow marsh where grasses bend and swish
A rainbow kite goes flying by, we watch a heron fish

We park our bike and climb a dune, below us, sparkling green...
"We're here!" I shout. "I'm king of the hill, my sister Meg's the queen!"

We're racing over ginger sand, our feet are hot hot hot hot!
"Quick, put the picnic blanket down." I find the perfect spot

We wade in right up to our knees, here comes a great big wave

Shivering, quivering, holding tight, we're trying to be brave

We're swimming — splishing, splashing — "Let's be porpoises and whales
Or pirates on a treasure hunt for mermaids' silvery scales"

First starfish, then we're jellyfish, drifting with the tide
Two tiny, briny urchins on a journey side by side

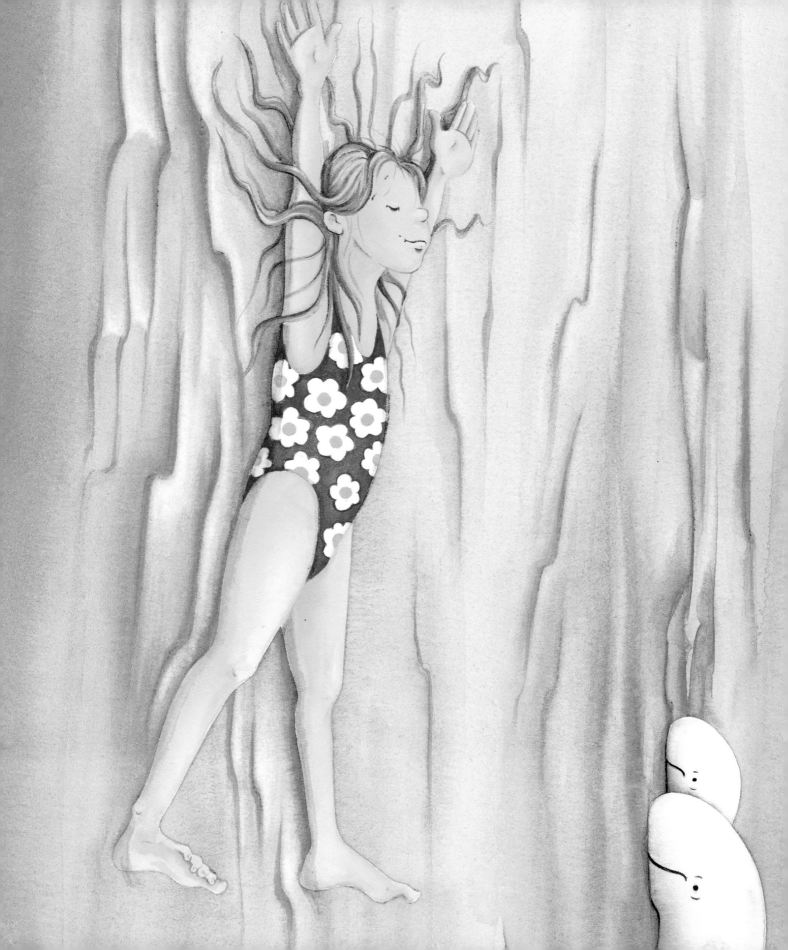

We're digging tunnels with our hands and making seaweed pies
While up above us cloud-sheep roam across blue summer skies

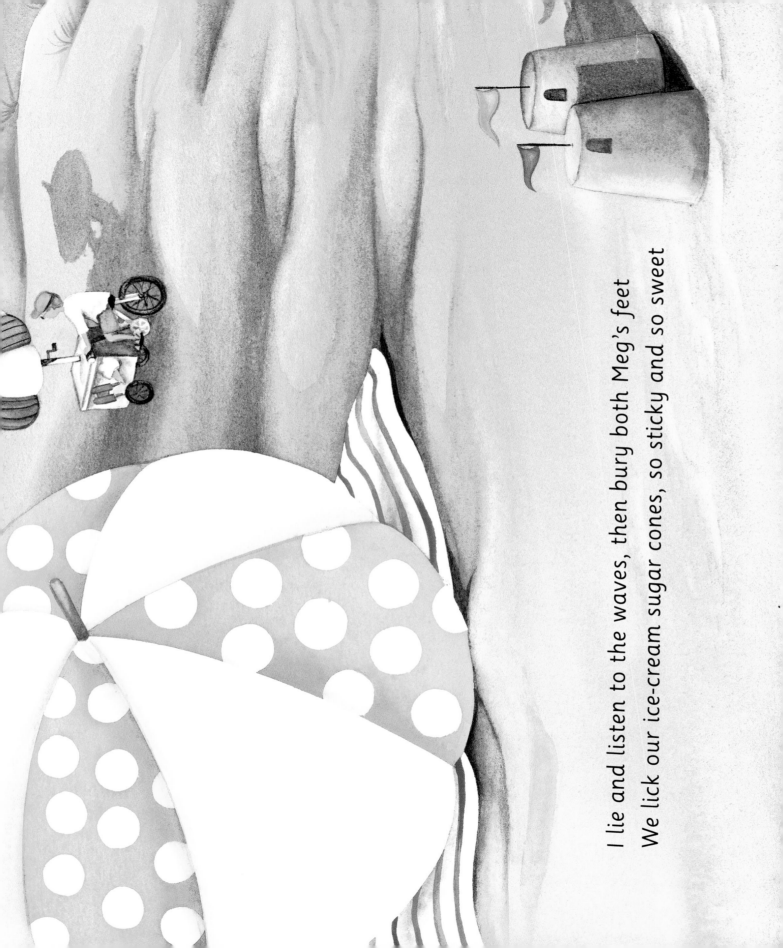

I lie and listen to the waves, then bury both Meg's feet

We lick our ice-cream sugar cones, so sticky and so sweet

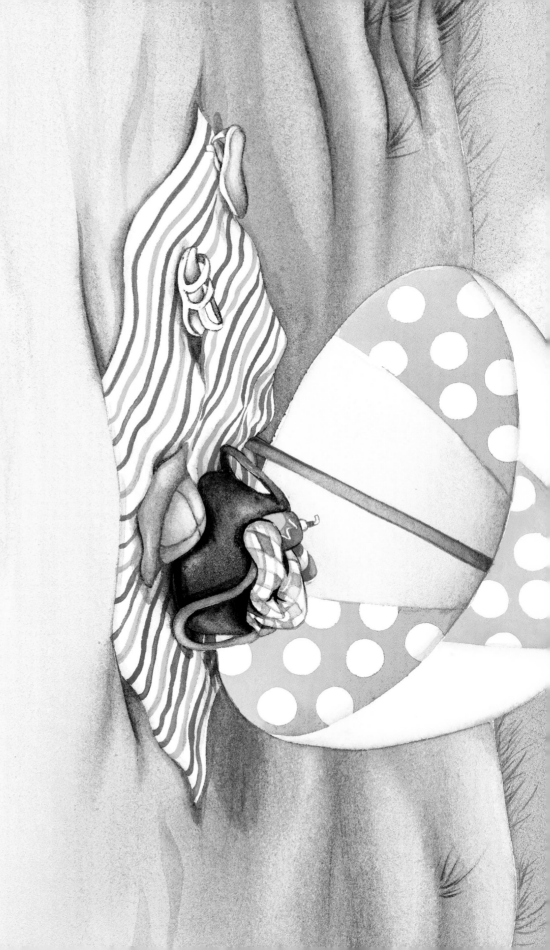

We're walking down the cool, wet beach, it's time to say goodbye
The sea tugs at our ankles as it heaves a salty sigh

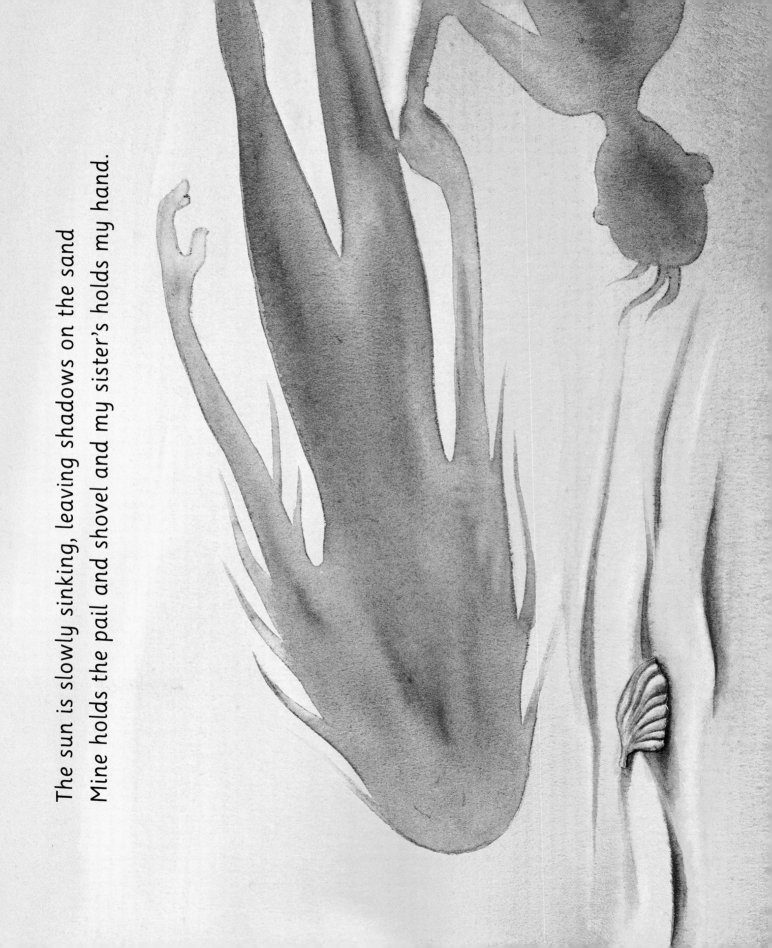

The sun is slowly sinking, leaving shadows on the sand
Mine holds the pail and shovel and my sister's holds my hand.

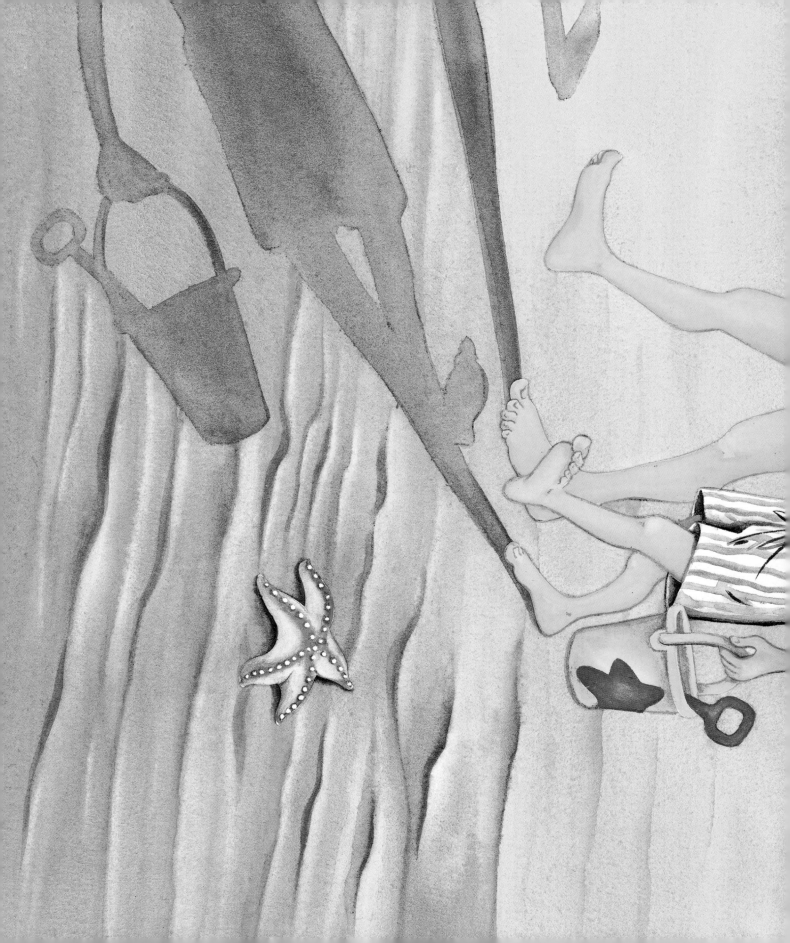

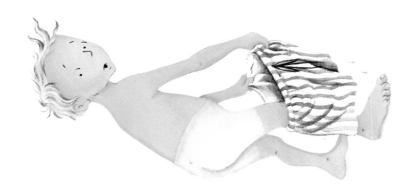